The Sleepover Club

Have you been invited to all these sleepovers?

1. The Sleepover Club at Frankie's
2. The Sleepover Club at Lyndsey's
3. The Sleepover Club at Felicity's
4. The Sleepover Club at Rosie's
5. The Sleepover Club at Kenny's
6. Starring the Sleepover Club
7. Sleepover Girls go Pop!
8. The 24-Hour Sleepover Club
9. The Sleepover Club Sleeps Out
10. Happy Birthday Sleepover Club
11. Sleepover Girls on Horseback
12. Sleepover in Spain
13. Sleepover on Friday 13th
14. Sleepover Girls go Camping
15. Sleepover Girls go Detective
16. Sleepover Girls go Designer
17. The Sleepover Club Surfs the Net
18. Sleepover Girls on Screen
19. Sleepover Girls and Friends
20. Sleepover Girls on the Catwalk
21. The Sleepover Club Goes for Goal!
22. Sleepover Girls go Babysitting
23. Sleepover Girls go Snowboarding
24. Happy New Year, Sleepover Club!
25. Sleepover Girls go Green
26. We Love You Sleepover Club
27. Vive le Sleepover Club!
28. Sleepover Club Eggstravaganza
29. Emergency Sleepover
30. Sleepover Girls on the Range
31. The Sleepover Club Bridesmaids
32. Sleepover Girls See Stars
33. Sleepover Club Blitz
34. Sleepover Girls in the Ring
35. Sari Sleepover
36. Merry Christmas Sleepover Club!
37. The Sleepover Club Down Under
38. Sleepover Girls go Splash!
39. Sleepover Girls go Karting
40. Sleepover Girls go Wild!
41. The Sleepover Club at the Carnival
42. The Sleepover Club on the Beach
43. Sleepover Club Vampires
44. sleepoverclub.com
45. Sleepover Girls go Dancing
46. The Sleepover Club on the Farm

by Fiona Cummings

An imprint of HarperCollins*Publishers*

First published in Great Britain by Collins in 2001
Collins is an imprint of HarperCollins*Publishers* Ltd
77-85 Fulham Palace Road, Hammersmith,
London, W6 8JB

The HarperCollins website address is
www.**fireandwater**.com

1 3 5 7 9 8 6 4 2

ISBN 0-00-711797-3

Printed and bound in Great Britain by
Omnia Books Limited, Glasgow

Sleepover Kit List

1. Sleeping bag
2. Pillow
3. Pyjamas or a nightdress
4. Slippers
5. Toothbrush, toothpaste, soap etc
6. Towel
7. Teddy
8. A creepy story
9. Food for a midnight feast:
   chocolate, crisps, sweets, biscuits.
   In fact anything you like to eat.
10. Torch
11. Hairbrush
12. Hair things like a bobble or hairband,
    if you need them
13. Clean knickers and socks
14. Change of clothes for the next day
15. Sleepover diary and membership card

CHAPTER ONE

Watch me, watch me, watch me!

Cool huh? I am Kenny, fantastic gymnastic! Did you see how I went straight from those cartwheels into a walkover-handstand combo? Wicked or what? I'll show you how to do it later if you want, but whatever you do, don't tell Fliss, OK? She thinks she's queen of the gymnastics scene, and once you get her started she'll show you her full repertoire of moves and you'll be there for *days*!

I guess when you think of gymnasts, you usually think of someone like Fliss, don't you? You know, all petite and bendy. You certainly wouldn't think of the rest of the Sleepover Club, that's for sure. I mean, Frankie is good at lots of sports, but petite she ain't! She's shooting up so fast that she's about as tall as King Kong now (though not as hairy!). Rosie's actually not bad at cartwheels and stuff, it's just that she's not completely confident in herself. So after every move, she stops to check that her leotard hasn't ridden up her bottom. And Lyndz, hmm – what can I say? Gymnastics and Lyndz just don't mix!

And me? Well, I'll give anything a go once. And although I'm too much of a tomboy to look all neat and tidy, I am pretty hot when it comes to the old gymnastic moves, even if I say so myself. (In fact I used to go to a gymnastics club, but Mum said I had to pack it in because I never had time to do my homework.)

So what's with all this gymnastic talk anyway, I hear you ask? Well, my little friend, you'd better sit down and make yourself comfortable because I have one wicked tale to tell. And it's not just about gymnastics either. Oh no. It's also about – and I'm going to whisper this next bit in case you're of a nervous disposition – *SATs.* You know exactly what I'm talking about, right? Those yucky, pukey, stupid tests that some cruel person devised as a form of torture for us poor children.

We've known since about Year One that this particular set of SATs was coming up, and Fliss has been panicking about them for just as long. You just have to mention the food chain, or percentages, and her eyes glaze over like you're talking a foreign language. She's been attending extra revision lessons with Lyndz and Rosie so they can push their scores up to the next level in the tests. I think it's just a question of giving them confidence really, and that's something Frankie and I certainly don't lack. It's not that we're brainboxes or swotty or anything. (Swotty? Me? Per-lease!) It's just that we don't get all jittery when we take tests. We go in there, do our stuff and come out again. Sorted!

Well, that's the theory anyway. This time it all went badly wrong. And by the time the SATs came round we were *all* under pressure – Big Time!

So you want to know how gymnastics came to be muddled up with SATs, do you? I guess I'd better start at the beginning, then.

OK, there were a few weeks to go before we sat the dreaded tests and all we seemed to hear was "SATs this" and "SATs that". We went over and over and over fractions and reading comprehension at school. Then we'd have to do revision on the solar system or something for homework. It was enough to make a girl reach for a jumbo-sized bag of Maltesers, I know that much. And if I remember rightly, that's exactly what I was doing when I saw the programme which just about changed our lives.

I went into the lounge and the local news was blaring out of the TV – yuckarama! That was so not what I needed to chill out with after all my hard work. But Mum and Dad were engrossed in it as usual so there was no way that I could turn it over to *The Simpsons*.

"Don't tell us you're actually going to sit down and watch this with us!" Mum looked shocked and pretended to faint.

"No way!" I mumbled. "Who wants to see all that boring stuff? If I wanted to depress myself I'd follow Molly around and watch her sad life."

I was referring to Molly my manky sister, in case you were confused. She's one incredibly gruesome geek, and I'm embarrassed I'm even related to her if you must know.

"Now now, Kenny, enough of that," Dad tutted. "Fortunately for you Molly's still at Carli's, but she'll be back any minute." He patted the empty cushion beside him on the sofa. "You really ought to start watching the news you know, Kenny. It's always a good thing to be aware of what's happening in the world around you. I know this is going to come as a terrible shock, but the entire universe doesn't revolve around you, your Sleepover chums and Leicester City Football Club."

"Oh no, Dad!" I collapsed dramatically next to him. "You mean there are other things out there too?"

Dad ruffled my hair and turned his attention back to the screen. To be absolutely honest with you, I was prepared to be bored out of my skull. I was even considering going back to my revision. But then up flashed this amazing footage of kids about my age doing these brilliant gymnastic routines. They were going from backflips into these wicked handstands where they actually did the splits in the air.

"Good gracious me!" Mum's eyes started to water. "That can't be good for you, can it?"

"Shh, Mum, I'm trying to watch," I hissed. I could feel Mum and Dad exchanging one of their looks over my head.

The presenter had now appeared on the screen. "Amazing, aren't they?" she smiled. "Well, gymnastics isn't only for Olympic hopefuls like these..."

There was a loud thud as Molly burst through the front door and dumped her bags in the hallway.

"Mum, there's someone at the door selling stuff," she called out. "Will you come and talk to him?"

Mum sighed and got up. Thanks to Molly I'd missed what the presenter was saying. I think it was something about gymnastics encouraging coordination and teamwork. I missed the next bit too because the phone rang.

"Dad, it's for you!" Molly yelled. "It's Mrs Davies about her piles!"

I couldn't believe it. The one time I was actually interested in something on the news, I couldn't hear a word because my stupid sister kept yelling at everybody. I went to sit on the carpet about a metre in front of the screen. And a good job I did too, because the presenter woman was just moving on to the interesting bit.

"... looking for raw talent. So we're organising a competition in the Leicester area to get all you 8- to 12-year-olds more involved. To make it fun we want you to get together with a group of up to five friends and work out a routine using some basic gymnastic moves. Each of you should perform a very short solo routine, and end by performing a routine all together. The music you choose is very important because it should enable you to express lots of different emotions. Now don't worry, we're not looking for anything like this..."

The film cut to a mind-blowingly complicated series of leaps, backflips and balances.

"What a load of prats!" Molly must have been watching from the doorway. "You wouldn't catch me prancing around like that."

"Well, seeing as you're as flexible as a tree trunk when you try to dance, I don't think there's much hope for you in gymnastics anyway," I grinned.

Molly made a lunge for my hair, but Mum came in and caught her just in time.

"Out you come, young lady. You can help me tidy up in the kitchen!"

I turned back to the television just in time to catch the presenter saying:

"The winners of our competition will become the stars of their very own TV series, which will follow their progress and see what kind of impact gymnastics has on their lives. Think *Popstars* in leotards! For more information send for our factsheet at the address which follows. And remember that the competition will be held on..."

But I didn't hear what she said next because I was flying out of the room looking for a pencil and paper so that I could copy down the address. This was just the kind of break the Sleepover Club was looking for. We're *always* looking for ways to get famous. (You've *got* to remember the time that Lyndz almost appeared in the advert for Spot Away spot cream.) I knew that the others would be totally razzed when I told them about it.

You know about the Sleepover Club, right? How we all stay over at each other's houses and have a laugh? Well, I started doodling all the names of the Sleepover Club on the piece of paper I was holding. I wrote Frankie's name first because we've known each other forever, and although we're not really supposed to have best friends in the club, she's mine. She's a real laugh and can go a bit crazy at times, but she's usually the one who makes sure we don't get too silly or carried away with our ideas. Next to her name I drew a star, because she's a star mate of course, but also because she's well into astrology and stuff.

"Is that in case you forget your friends' names?" Dad asked, glancing over my shoulder at the paper. Fortunately I'd folded it over so he couldn't see the address I'd written for the competition. "Why've you drawn a picture of a princess next to Fliss's name?"

"'Cos she thinks she is one, of course!" I giggled.

"There's nothing wrong with wanting to look nice," Dad said, eyeing my scruffy Leicester City football shirt.

"Yeah, but she takes it a bit far sometimes," I said, "bothering about her eyeshadow when we're supposed to be planning serious Sleepover business."

"Well, maybe it's to build up her confidence?" Dad suggested. "She might be feeling a bit pushed out now her mum's got the twins to worry about."

I guess he had a point. It must be kind of weird having babies in the house again when you get to our age. Although Frankie's got a new baby sister too and she hasn't gone all freaky over make-up and stuff. But then Fliss's mum is a bit, erm, neurotic at the best of times. I guess Fliss's life isn't as easy as we think it is.

"Now why does it not surprise me that you've drawn a picture of a horse next to

Lyndz's name?" Dad laughed, looking more closely at my piece of paper.

Everyone knows how mad Lyndz is about horses. I guess that's her escape from all four of her brothers – they're enough to make anyone crazy. But strangely enough, Lyndz is one of the calmest people you'll ever meet. She hates it when we fall out and is always playing the peacemaker. And she has the most fearsome hiccups in the world!

I drew one of those mask-type things next to Rosie's name – you know, the kind where one face is laughing and the other is crying.

"That's a bit of a strange thing to draw, Kenny." Dad looked puzzled. "What's that about?"

"Well, you never know what you're going to get with Rosie, do you?" I pointed out. "She's great fun most of the time, but sometimes she can be really prickly."

Finally I drew a football next to my name on the list. If there's one thing I'm passionate about it's Leicester City Football Club. As well as my friends, of course. Which is why I was determined that we should win this gymnastics competition. It would be a *major* thrill for all of us.

When Dad had gone out of the room, I started to seriously think about gymnastics and what we could do. And I was reminded of one thing – Circus Jamboree. Do you remember Ailsa trying to teach us how to perform flick-flacks? And the workshop we went to? Well I kind of wished I *hadn't* remembered it, because we weren't really much cop at all the acrobatic stuff. And this time, just dressing up as clowns wouldn't win us any prizes!

Still, hadn't the TV presenter said that for this competition they didn't want gymnastic geniuses, they wanted "raw talent"? Well, she wouldn't get talent much rawer than the Sleepover Club's, that was for sure. And I was pretty certain that when the others realised that the prize was to star in our very own television programme, they would be able to backflip and flick-flack with the best of them.

I went back up to my bedroom and started to practise a few moves. I did a couple of cartwheels but there wasn't as much room as I thought, and I crashed straight into Molly's bedside cabinet. A few of her precious ornaments fell over, so I picked them up quickly, because she goes ballistic if anyone even *looks* at her stuff.

Then I tried to do a handstand and make shapes with my legs in the air. But it's much harder than it looks and I ended up sprawled on the floor. Hmm, I could see that we would have to get in some serious practice if we were going to win this competition.

But that wasn't my biggest problem. No. I could hear Molly thudding upstairs like an elephant, so I had to get back to my homework. If there's one thing that Molly loves doing, it's winding me up about the SATs.

And sure enough, as soon as she came in she started.

"I hope you're working hard there baby sis, because those SATs papers are just the hardest thing ever!"

Molly sat hers last year so she reckons she knows everything about them now.

"And let's be honest," she carried on, "you're not as clever as me, are you? I mean, you'll never get the levels I got."

She smiled a false sickly smile. "But you've got to do your best, you know. And I promised Mum and Dad that I'd keep an eye on you and make sure that you're working hard. So no slacking now, Laura dearest. We can't have you letting the McKenzie family down, can we?"

Sometimes I could quite happily stuff my sister down a dirty toilet and flush her round the U-bend. But instead I flashed her a sarcastic smile and gritted my teeth. I had to keep the peace and make sure that she didn't find out about the competition, because if she did she'd make my life hell for sure.

The next morning I was bursting to tell the others about our chance to be famous. But I was kind of late for school, so they were already in the classroom when I managed to catch up with them.

"I've got some excellent news for you," I garbled as I plonked myself down at our table.

"Have the SATs been cancelled?" whispered Fliss hopefully.

But before I could reply, Mrs Weaver turned her beady eyes on me.

"I am trying to get on with registration, if that's all right with you, Laura?"

I absolutely HATE anybody using my real name, so I did my best impression of a very angry tomato.

After that there was no way that I could tell the others about the competition, especially as we had a maths test which we had to do in absolute silence. To be fair, I did try to give them as many clues as I could. Like drawing a picture of us on television on my paper. But they just thought I was doodling because I was bored. So 'accidentally on purpose' I dropped my rubber on the floor. And when I went to pick it up I did a weenie little handstand. Lyndz stared at me like I'd lost it completely, but Mrs Weaver was *not* impressed.

"Laura McKenzie, is there any particular reason for your foolish antics, or are you just too shy to ask me for the extra maths homework I am now going to give you?"

A ripple of giggles spread round the room.

At least the extra homework would be worth it when I told the others my news. They wouldn't just be giggling then. Oh no, they'd be whooping and cheering, carrying me on their shoulders and telling me how they'd be grateful to me forever for making them stars. Well, I expected something like that anyway. Boy was I in for a surprise!

"Gymnastics?" Frankie shrieked when I'd told them all my news. "I don't think so, Kenny. I mean, look at me. I don't exactly look like a gymnast, do I? Gymnasts are *small*. I'd be laughed out of the place for looking like a freak."

"But that's exactly the point of the competition," I assured her. "Gymnastics isn't just for delicate little people..."

"Like me!" piped up Fliss.

"Yep, like you Fliss. It's for everyone. They're trying to get more people to join in and benefit from it. Oh come on, it'll be fun. What do you think, Lyndz?"

Lyndz was looking pretty sick actually.

"I agree with Frankie," she said. "You know that I'm hopeless at gym, Kenny. I even get stuck on forward rolls sometimes. And do you remember that time Mrs Weaver asked us to try a handstand and I lost my balance and crashed down on top of Alana Banana? She was so dazed everyone thought she had concussion. She was off school for ages."

"But the presenter said each person only has to do a *short* solo performance, Lyndz," I reassured her. "There must be lots of gymnastic-type balances and stuff you *can* do. And the rest of us can cover for you when we do the routine all together."

"I suppose." Lyndz shuffled her feet and didn't sound too convinced.

"So Rosie-Posie, are you up for it?" I demanded.

Rosie smiled warily. "Yeah, I guess so. As long as it doesn't interfere with SATs too much. I've promised Mum I'm going to work really hard for these tests."

"When is the competition exactly?" Frankie wanted to know.

"Dunno," I shrugged. "Ages away, I think. Anyway, wouldn't it be great to have something to look forward to *after* the SATs? And in the meantime, practising for it will help us clear our minds a bit. What do you say?"

The others all looked at each other. Only Fliss was jumping about like she'd got ants in her pants.

"It'll be so cool!" Fliss twittered. "This competition was made for me… I mean, *us*!"

I sighed. I just knew that *that* was because she thought she was little and perfect and would capture the judges' hearts the moment they saw her. PUKE!

To be honest I was well cheesed off with the others. You'd think they could have mustered *some* enthusiasm when I was offering them the chance of stardom.

"Look guys, don't you realise that if we win this thing, we actually get to star in our own TV programme?" I told them in exasperation. "And that's not just going to be about gymnastics, is it? It's going to be about *us*. Everybody will get to see us and we'll be famous. Lyndz, they'll probably film you at Mrs McAllister's stables.

You'll be able to show everyone how much you love horses and you'll be offered some top job where you can ride the best horses in the world all day. Isn't that what you want?"

Lyndz's eyes had begun to sparkle. She beamed and nodded.

"And Frankie, you'll bowl everyone over with how witty and clever you are and no one will even notice that you're as tall as a giraffe!"

Frankie batted me playfully on the arm. But I could see that she was beginning to realise what a mega-opportunity we were looking at here.

"And I'll be spotted by a model agency, won't I? It's going to be *totally* cool!" Fliss gushed again. "It's a brilliant idea, Kenny. Have you sent off for the factsheet yet? We've got to start planning everything. I mean, I'm brilliant at gymnastics, but you knew that, right? I'm sure I can teach you all a few moves, even you Lyndz."

And with that she cartwheeled across the grass in front of us.

"Charming!" Lyndz tutted, but she was laughing really.

"So are we about to be famous TV stars then?" I shouted.

"YES!" the others chorused.

"We should start rehearsing right away!" Fliss reappeared, a little breathless from her exertion. "What about after school?"

"Revision!" the others reminded her.

"Who cares about stuffy old SATs when we're going to be on TV?" she retaliated.

"I think you're being just a tad hasty there, Fliss," Rosie reminded her. "We've got to actually *win* the competition first, you know."

But you could tell that there was no stopping Fliss now. She had that look on her face which spelt trouble with a capital T.

"Oh-oh, she's in Cloud Cuckoo Land again," Frankie whispered. And we just knew that Fliss's fluffy little brain was filling up with images of herself being mobbed by adoring fans whenever she went out. Revision for SATs was going to have a really tough time competing with that.

To be honest with you, it was hard enough finding time to see each other at all, what with after-school revision clubs and the masses of homework that Mrs Weaver kept piling on top of us. But as soon as I'd received the factsheet about the competition, we made a firm arrangement to meet round at my place.

"So how was the science revision club?" I asked as Lyndz, Rosie and Fliss staggered through the door.

"I just don't get it," Lyndz moaned. "I mean, reversible changes? What's that all about then?"

"Oh come on Lyndz, Mrs Weaver's been going on about it for the last hour. You've got to understand it by now!" Rosie sounded really exasperated. "Water turns into ice when it freezes, doesn't it? But you can melt ice when the conditions are warm enough, right? So that's a reversible change."

"And salt dissolves in water," added Frankie. "But you can recover it again through evaporation, so *that's* a reversible change too."

"But what about bread turning into toast?" Lyndz looked puzzled. "If you burn it, you can scrape the black bits off so it looks like bread again, can't you?"

"WHAT?" we all shrieked. "Changes involving burning are *never* reversible!"

Lyndz started spluttering.

"You're having a laugh, aren't you?" I yelled, wrestling Lyndz to the floor. "The question is, if I tickle you until you explode, what kind of change would that be, Lyndz?"

"An icky, gooey, horrible change!" giggled Rosie.

All the time we were fooling around, Fliss was stretching elaborately in the hallway, totally oblivious to us.

"What's with her?" Frankie asked, when Lyndz and I had finally picked ourselves up.

"I don't know," Rosie shook her head. "She was like that all the time in the class. She wasn't paying any attention at all."

"Yeah," Lyndz whispered, as we crept into the lounge. "I thought Mrs Weaver was really going to lose her rag at one point. It's like she's on another planet. Planet Gymtastic!"

"Planet TV Star more like," Frankie moaned. "That's all she went on about today. It's like everything else has just gone out of the window. And that's really weird because until you told us about that competition, Kenny, she'd been driving us all crazy by stressing so much about the SATs."

"Yeah, you're right," I agreed. "But now it's like she's forgotten all about them."

"Maybe she'll be OK once we've started practising," Lyndz suggested. "You know, maybe it's something she needs to get out of her system."

"Hey guys, shouldn't we be getting on with planning our routine?" asked Fliss, sticking her head round the door. "I mean, I know what *I'm* going to do for my bit, but we've got to get the rest of you looking decent as well, haven't we?"

We all burst out laughing and chased her into the garden.

Now when Lyndz had said that she was useless at gymnastics, she wasn't joking. You know when babies do that thing where they look as though they're going to do a forward roll, then collapse at the last minute? Well, Lyndz was just like that. And the more Fliss tried to encourage her to do a cartwheel, the funnier it got. First she just ended up doing strange, lopsided little bunny hops. Then she kicked Fliss in the arm as Fliss tried to help Lyndz's balance. And finally she ended up sprawled on her back in Dad's compost heap.

"Aw yuck, Lyndz, you stink!" Frankie held her nose.

"Sorry, hic, guys!" Lyndz gulped. "I, hic, told you I wasn't, hic, any good at this kind of, hic, stuff!"

"You'll get there Lyndz, it's just a matter of practice," Rosie reassured her, as she rubbed Lyndz's back to get rid of the dreaded hiccups. "Anyway Kenny, why don't we have a look at your factsheet now? There might be a few suggestions on moves which would be suitable for Lyndz."

"Good idea, Batman!" I agreed, racing up to my bedroom for the paper.

It did have some really helpful suggestions in it. And it described how in gymnastics the most important thing is the quality of the shapes you make with your body.

"There you go, Lyndz!" I grinned. "You could just stand at the back and make shapes. Like this!" I stood up and spread myself out like a starfish, then crouched down and stuck one arm in the air. The others doubled up in hysterics. Except Fliss.

"I don't think it means that at all," she sniffed. "But look, the bit about music is in bold type – that must be important."

"It says that 'gymnasts should choose music which enables them to express different emotions. Each move should be in tune with the music, and one move should move seamlessly into another.' Well, that's all right then!" I said, pulling a face. "What kind of music 'expresses different emotions'?"

"It doesn't, hic, mean classical music, does it?" wondered Lyndz. "I mean that, hic, would just put the icing on it if we had to, hic, prance around to that."

"They mean show tunes," Fliss announced smugly. "Gymnasts usually perform routines to songs from big musicals like *Phantom of the Opera* or *Miss Saigon*. Mum's got loads of CDs from shows, I'm sure she'll help us to pick some out."

"No way!" I told her firmly.

The others backed off. They knew what was

coming. We were winding up for another Kenny and Fliss showdown.

"You and your mum might like show tunes Fliss, but the rest of us don't," I continued."I couldn't even recognise a song from Miss Saigon if it bit me on the bottom. And just because other gymnasts use music like that, doesn't mean that we have to, OK?"

"I was only trying to help!" Fliss said huffily. "I want us to win this competition, that's all."

"Well so do I," I told her. "And that's why we're not going to tell our parents about the competition just yet. We're going to win this by doing things our way, OK?"

"OK," the others agreed.

But I could see by the look in Fliss's eyes that things weren't OK. Far from it. I'd never seen her looking so defiant before. It was almost like she was a different person.

The hairs pricked up on the back of my neck and a shiver crept down my spine. I knew then that this whole competition thing was going to bring us nothing but trouble. What I didn't know was just how much.

“Fliss has turned into a power-crazed freak!” Frankie flopped down on the lawn next to me. We were at her place after school, practising our gymnastic moves.

“She’s just been having a right go at me because I couldn’t hold my handstand long enough,” Frankie carried on. “I told her that it’s easy for her with her short little legs. Mine are so long it’s like trying to balance two drainpipes up there!”

“What did she say?”

Frankie put on her ‘prim Felicity Proudlove’ voice. “‘You must practise, practise, practise

Frankie. I've got my work cut out as it is trying to get Lyndz to look half-way decent.'"

We both dissolved into giggles.

"Poor Lyndz!" I chortled.

We both squinted into the distance, where Fliss was demonstrating to Lyndz how she wanted her to kneel, lift and stretch her left leg behind her then move into a forward roll. But every time Lyndz tried to follow her instructions, Fliss found something to complain about.

"No Lyndz, you must keep your leg straight."

"Tuck your *head* in, Lyndz, that looks so untidy."

Frankie and I pulled a face at each other.

"Come on, we'd better go and rescue her!"

We raced over to them. Rosie, who had been practising cartwheels and arabesques by herself, came to join us.

"I think we should call it a day, you guys," I suggested.

Lyndz looked at me gratefully.

"We really must sort out our music, you know," Fliss sniffed. "How can I choreograph anything until I know what music we'll be using?"

The rest of us stifled a few splutters.

"You can all come over to mine tomorrow," Fliss went on, ignoring us. "We've got masses of CDs, I'm sure we'll be able to find something."

"As long as it's not a show tune," I warned her.

I was getting seriously ticked off by the way Fliss was taking over this whole competition thing. Hadn't it been my idea that we entered it in the first place? And didn't I have some experience of gymnastics too?

"We'll see," Fliss sniffed. "There's no revision club tomorrow, so you can come straight after school."

"OK," we all agreed. But I, for one, wasn't looking forward to it.

I was looking forward to it even less after Mrs Weaver had broken her news to us in the afternoon.

"I want you to be as prepared as possible for the SATs in a couple of weeks' time," she announced, smiling as though she'd just told us that she was taking us to the seaside as a treat. "So the day after tomorrow we're going to have a mock science test under exam conditions. Now I know you've all been working very hard already, but it might be a good idea to put in a little extra revision over the next two nights."

We all groaned and started pulling faces at each other.

"We have covered all the work," Mrs Weaver continued. "So this is just a chance to get used to the kinds of questions you will be faced with in the proper tests. All right?"

But everyone was grim-faced and silent.

"I won't be able to stay long, Fliss," Lyndz told her as we were walking to Fliss's house. "I need all the help I can get when it comes to science tests."

"Yeah, I need to go through all that solar system stuff," Rosie admitted. "I get kind of muddled up about what orbits what."

"I guess we all need to revise tonight," Frankie agreed. "We'll just come in for half an hour, choose our music, and then get home, OK?"

"I suppose," Fliss shrugged her shoulders. "I wish we could practise for the gymnastics competition instead. Revision is just *so* boring!"

"Felicity Proudlove! I don't believe what I just heard," a voice piped up from Fliss's garden. We couldn't see anyone but there was no mistaking that voice. It was Fliss's mum! And if she'd heard about the gymnastics competition, we were dead!

We trooped into the garden as Mrs Proudlove, who had been playing with her baby twins Joe and Hannah, launched forth.

"You know how important these SATs are, Felicity. Of course you have to revise for them. I know that you're a clever girl, but you've got to get the marks to prove it. I want you to do well, sweetie, but you have to work for it. Now, you girls can stay for a drink and a biscuit, but then I really think you should run along home and start revising too. The SATs are only a few weeks away now, you know."

"Blimey!" I gasped as we went inside. "What's your mum like, Fliss? Is she hyper or what?"

"She just wants me to do well, that's all," said Fliss defensively, and poured us all a glass of lemonade. I swigged mine down in one and burped loudly.

"Kenny!" Frankie pretended to be shocked.

"It's only 'cos it was so gassy," I grinned. "Well, come on then. Let's get this show on the road!"

We piled into the lounge and began pulling CDs from the carefully organised rack. Fliss was right when she said they had loads. The trouble was, they were all naff.

"Per-lease!" Rosie screeched after we'd listened to some big fat guy singing opera.

"No way!" Lyndz insisted after about a million snippets of classical music.

"Absolutely not!" Frankie and I agreed when Fliss had run through the highlights of her famous show tunes. "There's got to be something we all like."

"What about a pop song?" Rosie suggested, and did a handstand whilst trying to sing *Don't Stop Movin'*.

"That's quite impressive, Rosie," Frankie admitted. "But somehow I don't think it's quite what the judges are looking for. The music has got to suggest a wide range of emotions. Besides, we've done our 'S Club 5' act in public before, remember!"

We all grinned as we remembered our recent success in the school dance competition.

"We'll just have to go away and think about it some more," said Lyndz, getting up and gathering her things together. "I really will have to go home now and get down to some serious revision."

We all got ready to go.

"But guys, what about the music? You promised!" Fliss whined. "I don't think any of you are taking this competition seriously at all."

"'Course we are," Rosie tried to soothe her. "It's just that we've got this test to get through first."

By that time we were at the front door, and Andy, Fliss's stepdad, had just driven up. Music was blaring out of his van, and Mrs Proudlove was going ballistic because she said it was disturbing the twins.

"Rubbish my love," Andy grinned. "The sooner they get used to a bit of Guns N' Roses the better. You don't get more emotion in a song than this." He cranked up the volume. "Axl Rose used to be my idol, girls," he shouted across to us. "He even looked good in a skirt!"

"Lovely!" I smiled at him. Then I whispered to the others, "Sounds a bit odd to me."

But there was something about the music he was playing that really got me. It was quiet and then got louder, swept into this amazing rhythmic section and then slowed down again.

"What is that music anyway?" I asked.

"It's called *Live and Let Die*," Andy replied. "Do you want to borrow the CD?"

"Nonsense, of course she doesn't," Fliss's mum complained. "If she wanted any version of this song, you'd want the one by Wings, wouldn't you Kenny?"

To be honest I had absolutely no idea what she was talking about. I'd never heard of Wings but then I'd never heard of Guns N' Roses either.

"Hmm," I said slowly. "Do you think you

could play that track again, Andy? From the beginning?"

Mrs Proudlove looked confused. Fliss, Rosie and Lyndz were looking at me as though I'd completely lost the plot too, but Frankie was nodding.

"Yeah, I'd like to hear it again as well."

"You see, I'll make you all metal heads yet!" Andy grinned. He flicked the CD back to the start of the track, closed his eyes and started to sing along.

It has to be said that the singer, that Axl Rose bloke, didn't have the greatest voice in the world – it was all scratchy and strained. But it was just perfect for the song.

Frankie and I hummed along to the bits we remembered. Then, when the rhythm and pace wound up, we started leaping about the driveway. I did a cartwheel and almost knocked Mrs Proudlove flying.

"Really, Kenny!" she gasped, jumping out of the way. "I think this music is doing funny things to you. Andy, look what you've done! And I'm sure that's Joe crying. Can you please turn the wretched thing down?"

With that she stomped up the path and into the house. Oops.

"This is fantastic! Perfect!" Rosie yelled as she tried to do one of those flying leaps across the rose bed.

"Isn't it great!" I shouted back.

"Well, you're the funniest Bond girls I've ever seen!" Andy guffawed. "I don't remember anyone doing those kinds of moves in the film."

"What film?" Lyndz asked.

"What do you mean, *what film*?" Andy sounded amazed. "The original Wings track was the theme tune for the Bond film, *Live and Let Die*. It was a bit before your time, I guess," he shrugged.

"James Bond's – always doing – gymnastic kind of moves, isn't he?" Frankie clutched her side as she gasped for breath. "This music is just the best!"

Fliss, who had been practising a few moves herself, rushed over to join the rest of us. As the music faded away we all hugged each other and started dancing round.

"We've found our music, we've found our music!"

Andy looked really puzzled. But at least he wasn't like Fliss's mum, who would have questioned us non-stop about what we were doing. We managed to fob him off with a story about the track being for PE and the gymnastics competition wasn't mentioned at all. At last, we'd got our music sorted out. All we needed now was the routine. And that was when things really started to go pear-shaped.

You see, the thing was that all Fliss could talk about were the blimming routines she'd so cleverly choreographed for us all. Like we'd got down on our knees and begged her to do it or something.

"I spent all yesterday evening working them out," she announced the next day.

"What about your revision?" asked Lyndz.

"Oh, you know, I did bits. But look, what do you think about this routine? Cool huh?"

By the time Fliss had shown us the moves she'd worked out for us all, it was obvious that this was *not* going to be a team effort. Fliss very definitely saw herself as the star – as usual.

"I've made you all a copy of *Live and let Die*," she announced, handing them out. "So next time we get together to rehearse I'll expect you all to know what you're doing."

As soon as her back was turned I started pulling gruesome faces. Unfortunately Fliss turned round and caught me.

"What's that for?" she asked, going all red in the face.

"I'm just a bit sick of you taking over the whole competition thing," I told her. "I found out about it, didn't I? But suddenly it's Felicity Proudlove turning into Miss Bossy Britches and telling us what to do. *As usual.*"

Fliss glared at me. "If you remember, it was Andy who had the CD *you* decided we wanted," she said. "I don't recall much discussion about whether we should use it or not. You decided and that was that."

"Well, you didn't raise any objections!" I spat back. "If it had been up to you we'd have been prancing about to one of your mother's favourite show tunes."

Fliss went even redder in the face and looked as though she was about to cry.

"We do all agree that it's the right music," Lyndz said soothingly. "And it was really good of Fliss to make us all a copy. It'll make it a lot easier for us to plan our routines."

"I don't think anyone's really in charge, are they?" Frankie suggested. "It's got to be a group effort. That's the whole point."

The others all nodded. I just grunted. I knew what Fliss was like. She thought she was this graceful little thing who everybody'd be looking at, so she assumed it was her right to take over. Well, I wasn't having that.

"I'll show you Felicity Proudlove!" I vowed.

I didn't *intend* to start planning gymnastic routines during the mock science test, I swear. It just sort of happened. I'd been playing *Live and Let Die* over and over as I revised the previous evening, and it had kind of got stuck in my head. So as soon as we turned our papers over and I recognised one of the questions, it started racing around again.

I tried to ignore it, I really did. But it was hard. Especially when one of the questions on forces and gravity gave me this brilliant idea for a whole series of really wicked moves for our finale together. I started sketching the whole thing out and just lost track of time. Instead of writing in answers about the life cycle of a plant or the human skeleton, I was jotting down plans for balances and leaps.

I was well pleased with the routine I'd drawn up, and started performing it with my fingers across the desk. I was sort of aware that Frankie was staring at me, but I just thought it was because she wanted to know what I was doing.

When I looked over at her, she had this look of anger and panic all mixed up across her face. Then she started doing this mad thing with her eyes. She stared hard at me, stared hard at the paper on my desk, then looked frantically at the clock on the wall. I tried to look back at her with question marks in my eyes like they do in cartoons, but that didn't work. It was only when I looked at the clock too that I realised what she was trying to tell me. There were only ten minutes to go and I still had most of the paper to complete!

What a nightmare! My brain was in a major fog from all the leaps I'd been planning, and it was kind of hard to flip out of gymnastics mode and back on to science. When I tried to read the questions, the words didn't seem to make any sense at all. It was as though they were written in Martian or something.

A question about the solar system threw me completely. Two days ago I'd understood the solar system like the back of my hand, but now it was complete nonsense. And the more I struggled over the questions, the less I could remember. In the end I didn't even have time to read them properly. I just latched on to a word or two that I recognised and stuck down the first answer I could think of.

"What on earth were you doing in there?" Frankie squeaked as soon as we came out.

But before I could answer, I had to frantically jot down my brilliant idea for the routine, because of course I'd had to hand it in on my answer sheet.

"We want to win this competition, don't we?" I asked when I'd finished. "And I had this brilliant idea for our routine. Look." I showed her my scruffy notes. "Honestly Frankie, it's better than anything Fliss can come up with. She'd be having us do little pirouettes and stuff, but this is brilliant and it'll go with our music perfectly!"

Frankie stared at me. "So basically all that in there was to get one over Fliss?"

"No. Well, all right then, I suppose it was," I admitted. "It's just that it was me who found out about the competition, and it really bugs me that she's starting to take over."

"Well I hope you feel proud of yourself!" Frankie yelled. "It's only a competition, you know. Who cares which of you came up with the routine? It's a bit of a laugh. If we win it, great. If we don't, it's not the end of the world. But it *will* be the end of the world if you mess up your work just because of some stupid feud with Fliss!"

I had to agree that she was right. I felt ashamed of myself for getting so carried away and I was determined to put everything back into perspective.

"I really will work hard for my SATs," I promised Frankie. "Then it'll be great to let off some steam when they're over by rehearsing for the competition, won't it?"

But I didn't know that it was too late. We were about to be hit by two of the biggest bombshells imaginable. And they were going to scupper all of our dreams for sure.

CHAPTER FOUR

You know how sometimes everything is going along just perfectly? You haven't a care in the world (apart from SATs and of course Fliss bossing everyone around for the competition) and then BAM! Something happens which turns your world upside down. Well, that's what happened to us just a couple of days after the mock science exam.

We were all round at my place trying to get our gymnastics routine together, and Fliss and I had been at each other's throats all night. She'd been acting the big cheese like she knew everything there was to know about handstands and backflips. You'd think she already had an Olympic medal for gymnastics, for goodness sake.

At least we had a laugh when she tried to put Lyndz through her paces. Frankie and I were almost hysterical. I mean, poor Lyndz was trying her best, but she just didn't look right at all.

"You look more like a constipated chicken than a gymnast!" I yelled out.

"Well you don't look too great yourself," Fliss shouted back. "Your posture's all wrong. Look, you should do your walkover like this."

She stood up straight, flung her arms in the air dramatically, and did a perfect walkover, finishing with a flourish like they do in the Olympics.

"We'll see about that!" I snapped and did TWO walkovers followed by a cartwheel.

"Follow *that* Miss Prissy-Flissy!" I goaded her.

"This isn't getting us anywhere," Frankie said sternly. "I'm going to look through that factsheet again to see if there are any more tips to make things a bit easier for us."

I pointed to where the factsheet was on the step, and carried on cartwheeling around the garden.

Suddenly there was a mammoth groan. Frankie was sitting there as white as a sheet with her hand over her mouth.

"What's up? You're not gonna hurl, are you?" I asked, rushing over to her.

She just shook her head and wafted the factsheet in front of our noses.

"Look at the date of the competition," she moaned. "It says it's on Saturday May 18th!"

We all looked at each other and shrugged.

"It's not your birthday, 'cos you've only just had it," I said slowly. "And the rest of our birthdays are ages away."

I pulled a silly face at the others, but they were all looking really sick as well. In fact, I was sure that Fliss was going to burst into tears at any minute.

"Come on! It can't be anything *that* important, surely?" I reasoned.

"Oh stop being so thick, Kenny! Even *you* must know what's happening two days later!" Rosie snapped angrily. "You remember SATs, those horrible examy things we've been revising for forever? Well, they start on the 20th. There's no way that our parents are going to let us enter this competition now."

"I don't understand it," said Lyndz quietly. "Why hadn't we noticed the date before?"

"The page with it on had got stuck to the one above," Frankie explained in a tight little voice. "With what looks like peanut butter."

The others all looked at me accusingly.

"You can't begrudge a girl a little snack now and then," I joked. But for once, jokes weren't going to get me out of this mess.

"There must be something we can do," I said at last. But I knew I was kidding myself. Whichever way you looked at it, we were doomed from ever entering the gymnastics competition.

"Unless..." Fliss suddenly piped up excitedly. "... Unless we told our parents that we were revising at each other's houses, met in Cuddington, caught the bus into Leicester, entered the competition and came home. That would work, wouldn't it?"

Her eyes were gleaming wildly and she was

jabbering on like a wild woman. I was gobsmacked. This was Fliss, Miss Goody-Two-Shoes herself, actually suggesting we do something *deceitful*! I mean, the very same thought had actually crossed *my* mind, but I knew that there was *no way* we could get away with it. I was actually quite proud of Fliss for being so daring. There was hope for her yet!

"It just wouldn't work, Fliss," Frankie told her gently. "You know as well as we do that the chances of us entering this competition have just melted to zero."

Well, Fliss did dissolve into tears then, and boy didn't we all know about it. We had to make up some stupid story for my mum about her being totally stressed about the SATs. It was true in a way, but not in the way Mum thought.

The next couple of days we walked around like we'd been told that all holidays had been cancelled forever, television had ceased to exist and the only music we'd ever be able to listen to would be Fliss's mum warbling along to her show tunes. And if you thought *that* was bad, it was about to get much MUCH worse.

You remember that mock science test we'd done? I must admit that I'd forgotten about it as well, until Mrs Weaver announced gravely:

"I'm sure you'll all be thrilled to know that I've marked your science tests."

A huge groan went round the classroom.

"You might well groan," she continued in a stony voice. "I felt like groaning myself when I saw some of the test papers. Some of you did extremely well..."

The M&Ms (arch-enemies, urgh) grinned at each other like Cheshire cats.

"... whilst others of you didn't. I have to say that I was very shocked when I saw some of the papers." Mrs Weaver gazed deliberately over at Fliss and me. We both blushed like beetroots and stared at the table.

"Now, before I speak to you individually, we will all go over the correct answers."

Talk about embarrassing. I couldn't even remember seeing the questions before, never mind remember what I'd put for the answers. It's a wonder I'd got any of them right at all.

The annoying thing was that I knew nearly all the answers as Mrs Weaver was going through them. Why had I been so distracted by our gymnastics routine? I felt really ashamed when she handed back my paper and I saw great big crosses all over it.

Just as the bell went for break she plonked her bottom down on my desk.

"I think we need to talk, Laura," she said seriously.

Oh-oh, trouble! As soon as she'd dismissed everyone else she launched forth in her "very concerned" tone of voice.

"You know Laura, I was very shocked when I marked your paper. I had no idea that you were struggling with science. I get the impression that perhaps it's the whole concept of the examination situation which you find hard. Your paper certainly gave the impression of someone who wasn't very focused on the subject. In fact, I'd say that you were positively distracted. Is that fair comment, do you think?"

I nodded and looked at my feet. I could hardly admit that my mind had been focused on planning a routine for a gymnastics competition, could I?

Mrs Weaver frowned. "Well, I think the best plan is to learn from this experience and attend a few revision sessions to settle you down before the SATs proper. I'll give your mother a call now and ask for her permission. Right then, off you go and enjoy the rest of break."

I was doomed with a big fat D. Sure, my mum had already given me the speech about trying my best. You know the one: "All we want is for you to try your best. Results aren't important, it's trying your best that matters, blah, blah, blah." You've had that one too, right? Well they don't mean it, do they? What they mean is, "get good marks, or else!"

So it was with a heavy heart that I went home that evening. I was expecting fireworks and I certainly wasn't disappointed. Mum went absolutely ballistic. And it didn't help that Molly had already opened her mouth and rammed her Nike trainers right in it. It turned out that she knew all about the competition because she'd found the factsheet in our room. Not only that, but she'd been taking sneaky peeks at our rehearsals too. And as she was already well cheesed off because I'd broken one of her precious ornaments whilst I was trying to do those backflips upstairs, she'd wasted no time in dobbing me in.

"Really, Laura," Mum said in her quiet but extremely angry voice. "I used to think that you were quite intelligent, but now I'm beginning to wonder. To waste your talents on some gymnastics competition when your SATs tests are just around the corner is stupid in the extreme. How many times must I tell you that however important it is to have interests, at this stage of your life your education must come first?"

(Yawn, yawn, heard it all before.)

"And if you persist in looking at me with that insolent expression on your face I'll make sure the Sleepover Club is disbanded forever, do I make myself clear?"

Man! Mum sure can bring you back to earth and make you feel about a centimetre high sometimes. By the time I'd promised her that I was going to get down to some serious work for the SATs, and that I definitely wouldn't be wasting any more time even *thinking* about the gymnastics competition, I felt like an old chewed up piece of Hubba-Bubba gum.

But if I thought *I'd* had a rough deal, it was nothing compared to Fliss. She was in a right state at school the next morning. Apparently Mrs Proudlove had exploded so far into the stratosphere that they thought they might have to launch a rocket just to bring her back.

"Mrs Weaver told Mum how disappointed she'd been with my test paper, and Mum just went mad," Fliss sobbed. "She kept going on and on about how hard it was for her looking after me and Callum and the twins and said that she couldn't cope with any more traumas. She really flipped, it was awful!"

Frankie put a reassuring arm round her. "I'm sure she was just upset at the time. She'll have calmed down now."

"I don't think so," Fliss sighed. "You should have seen her. She kept going on and on about how I'd let her down, and how I was wasting my brain and how sorry I'd be if I messed up my exams and ended up in a dead-end job."

Now that did seem a bit dramatic. After all, it was only one little test Fliss had messed up on.

"And she said I'd be grounded for life if I didn't put in some serious work!" Fliss wailed.

Oooh, nasty!

"The thought of being stuck in with your mum on the rampage for the rest of my days would make me get down to some pretty serious revision!" I laughed.

I thought that was funny, but no one else did. They all gave me really weird looks and carried on trying to comfort Fliss.

"I guess what Kenny is trying to say, in her clumsy way" – Frankie flashed me a look – "is that maybe we should *all* work hard and forget about the gymnastics competition. Our exams are more important, and the olds won't ever think differently. Agreed?"

"Agreed!" we all nodded glumly.

So, all in all the next few days were boring in the extreme. Imagine watching paint dry whilst listening to nursery rhymes all day long and you still don't come close to how boring our lives were. We went to school, we worked, we came home and did yet more work. We ate and we went to bed. Then the next day we got up and did exactly the same things again. I told you it was boring.

But before *you* get really bored and decide to leave me here talking to myself, I'm going to tell you about the miracle that happened which cheered us all up. And you'll never guess what it was. Not even if I promise you a triple fudge sundae with extra sauce on top. Well… go on then, try to guess!

Have you given up yet? No, the SATs weren't cancelled due to lack of interest. And you're wrong again if you think that our parents went down on bended knees to apologise and begged us to enter the competition after all. Now that *would* have been cool. No, the miracle which saved the day for us was... Look, I'll tell you how I found out about it, shall I? Then everything will become clear.

It was after another boring day at school (surprise, surprise) and I'd gone home and dug out my books on science to do yet more revision. You see what a good girl I am!

Anyway, after I'd read through details of the solar system about a million times and filled in a factsheet Mrs Weaver had given us for homework, my *head* was in a spin, never mind all those planets. I figured what I needed was a nice chocolate milkshake to settle my brain cells down again. So I headed down to the kitchen to make one.

Mum was listening to some dweeby programme on the radio. You know the kind where some sad geezer spends half an hour chatting to an old crumbly, then plays a song which was last in the charts when Queen Victoria was on the throne.

"Hello love. Are you having a break?" Mum asked, brushing flour from her hands. She's a wicked baker is my mum, and I was pleased to see that she'd knocked up one of her yummy pies for supper.

But all thoughts of food went right out of my head when I heard what was on the radio. The newsreader was explaining very seriously about the chaos which had occurred in Leicester that afternoon due to a major flood in the Community Hall.

Now I know that isn't exactly earth-shattering news, and to be honest it didn't mean much at all to start with. Until the newsreader went on to say that all functions which were due to take place there over the next few weeks would have to be rearranged whilst the hall was cleared out and the damage assessed.

Suddenly my little grey cells began to whir into action. I remembered that the *gymnastics competition* was due to be held at the Community Hall. That certainly couldn't happen now, could it? There was just a glimmer of hope that we might be able to enter it again. Unless it was going to be held somewhere else on the same day...

I had to wait until the local evening news on TV to find out. All the time I was waiting I felt sick. I couldn't even manage much of Mum's pie and that really worried her. She kept looking at me anxiously and asking me if I'd been overdoing my work. Classic!

The news about the Community Hall finally came on, and the reporter made a big deal about the gymnastics competition being cancelled there, because of course the TV company was sponsoring it.

"So now there will be *three* heats for the competition," the reporter announced. "And the winners of each will go through to a grand final. The heats will be held at Shalton Town Hall, Knaresby Community Rooms and Cuddington Leisure Centre…"

Cuddington Leisure Centre! I couldn't believe what I'd just heard. I tried to focus on what she was saying next and I started praying that the heats wouldn't still be held on Saturday 18th May.

"… and all the heats will now take place on Saturday 1st June."

"Yes! Yes! Yes!" I started leaping round the room, punching the air.

Molly walked past and snarled, "Saddo!" but I didn't care, I was just so thrilled. It was like a sign that we *had* to enter the competition. It was as though we were destined to win it!

And that's just what Frankie and Fliss thought when I told them too.

"It's amazing!" Frankie agreed when I phoned her. "Our parents have just *got* to let us enter it now."

"Yeah, but you know what happened last time."

"What happened to you and Fliss, you mean," Frankie reminded me. "The rest of us managed not to get so carried away, thank you very much."

She had a point there.

"We'll have to stay cool this time," I warned Fliss when I spoke to her later. "SATs have to come first, OK? At least that way we'll keep our parents off our backs and they'll have no reason to stop us entering the competition."

"Yeah, 'course," Fliss agreed breezily. "But isn't it cool that the date's moved? It's like the flood happened just so we could enter it again, isn't it?"

"Yep, you feel like the television programme already has our name on it, don't you?" I giggled. "*Sleepover Club: Gymnastic Stars*! does have a certain ring…"

Rosie and Lyndz had already heard the

news when I phoned them. Neither of them seemed that excited, to be honest. Rosie tends to be quite cool about stuff anyway, and doesn't get as wound up as the rest of us. But I think poor Lyndz had actually been relieved when the dates had clashed last time. Now she'd have to start practising her gymnastic moves all over again.

Still, when we got to school the next day, the competition was all we could talk about.

"We've been given this chance again, so we've just got to make it count," I told the others seriously. "We'll have to get some serious practice in, 'cos don't forget we've already missed valuable rehearsal time."

I did a couple of walkover-cartwheel combos just to prove that I hadn't lost my touch. Then Fliss joined me in her routine of arabesque, handstand, walkover and stag leap.

"Way to go, Fliss!" I applauded her. I mean, I know she was showing off and everything, but she did look like a pretty mean gymnast. And besides, if we both performed like that in the competition there was no way we were going to lose. Even if Lyndz did look about as elegant as a chimpanzee with tummy-ache when she did her routine.

"We really ought to get our parents' permission this time, you know," Rosie suggested. "I mean, there's no point getting all geared up for the competition again if they completely refuse to let us enter it."

She had a point, but I felt a bit queasy just thinking about it. After all, I had messed up my mock science test, hadn't I? And Mum had been pretty scary when she'd warned me about my education coming first. I'd just have to prove to her that I was serious about working for the SATs.

"We might as well get it over with and see what they say this evening," Frankie decided. "As my gran always says, there's no time like the present."

I tried not to think about what would happen if Mum absolutely refused to let me join in the competition. And I could tell that Fliss was getting pretty worked up about asking *her* mum too. My mum is like Snow White compared to Mrs Proudlove – she can be like the Wicked

Witch of the West in stilettos even on a *good* day!

Before we went our separate ways that afternoon, we had a group hug.

"Remember, we've got to enter this competition if we're going to be TV stars," I told the others severely. "So go out there and do some *serious* grovelling, do you understand?"

"We understand," they nodded solemnly.

"Sleepover Club rules!" I yelled.

"Sleepover Club rules!" they repeated and we all leapt in the air and did high fives.

So I was feeling pretty pumped up when I got home. But finding the right moment to ask Mum about the competition was harder than I'd expected. The one thing I did know was that I didn't want Molly the Monster anywhere near me when I was doing my grovelling. For one thing she'd never let me forget it if she heard me, and for another, she'd be sure to start stirring it with Mum. But wouldn't you know it? That particular evening was the one she'd chosen to come over all goody-goody by doing her homework in our room. She didn't even leave me alone for a minute to go to the bathroom, for goodness sake.

I had planned to build up to asking Mum about the competition by telling her how well I'd been doing in the revision classes and showing her all the revision I'd done by myself. But that had to go completely out of the window. Instead I had to grab my opportunity the minute Molly's mate Carli rang up after supper.

Mum was in the kitchen washing up by herself, so I grabbed a tea towel and started to help her.

"All right, what do you want?" she smiled.

"Aw Mum, nothing... well, there is something actually," I spluttered.

"Now why does that not surprise me?" Mum grinned. "Go on then, what is it?"

"WellgymnasticscompetitionwasbeforeSATs nowaftersocanweenterit?"

I couldn't believe what rubbish had just come out of my mouth. It was like my brain was working too fast for my mouth and my tongue had somehow got stuck to my teeth.

"Do you think you could say that again? In English this time," Mum asked.

I explained how the date of the competition had been changed and how we were all working really hard for our SATs.

"We won't even *think* about gymnastics until after the tests, I promise – cross my heart and hope to die!" I told her very solemnly.

Mum looked at me steadily. "Hmmm, Laura. Can I believe you, I wonder?"

"Aww Mum! 'Course you can," I pleaded. "I really want to do well in these tests. And you can ask Mrs Weaver how hard I've been working if you don't believe me."

"Well actually, I don't need to do that," Mum said lightly. "I saw her yesterday and she told me how pleased with you she was. In fact she remarked how all of your friends were really buckling down to some hard work. I must say I felt quite proud of you!"

I rushed over to her and gave her a big hug.

"Does that mean you'll let me enter the competition then?"

"Yes…"

"YESSSS!" I punched the air, then grabbed her and did a dance around the kitchen.

"… as I was saying," Mum carried on when I'd finally stopped spinning her round. "You can enter it *only* if you promise to get your SATs out of the way *before* you start planning your routines."

"Of course," I nodded. Most of the routines were planned anyway, weren't they? So a week should be long enough to perfect them before the competition.

A sudden burst of inspiration struck me.

"How about a revision sleepover to set us on our way before the SATs?" I asked cheekily. "We haven't had one for ages and it would really calm us down."

"We're way ahead of you there, my girl!" Mum slapped me playfully with her wet dishcloth. "I've spoken to all your friends' mums and we agreed that as you'd put in such a lot of hard work recently you could have a sleepover the Friday before the tests start."

"Mum you're brilliant!" I gave her a Kenny Special until she was gasping for air. "Is it going to be here then?"

"Erm, not exactly." Mum sat down to get her breath back. "It'll be with Nikki and Andy."

I started to protest but Mum put her hand up.

"Felicity's mum wasn't too keen on the idea at first. The only reason she agreed was because if you had it there, she could keep an eye on you." Mum looked at me apologetically.

Ah well, a sleepover at Fliss's was better than no sleepover at all, wasn't it? We could still have fun, couldn't we? Well, couldn't we?

Now, as you must know by now, sleepovers at Fliss's aren't the most relaxing in the world. The thing is, Mrs Proudlove isn't really geared up to our sort of fun. She expects us to sit down and be ladylike at all times. You know the kind of thing,

"I say Felicity darling, would you be so good as to pass me one of those spiffing cream cakes?"

"Oh absolutely, Kenny old bean. I say, they really are sooper-dooper scrumptious!"

Pukerama! And of course, by the time this sleepover came round we were all a bit frazzled after so much revision, not to mention totally hyper because the dreaded SATs were almost upon us. Plus we knew that the gymnastics competition was looming up too. PHEW! It makes you exhausted just *thinking* about it, doesn't it?

Anyway, on the Friday evening we all piled round to Fliss's, clutching not only our sleeping bags and sleepover kit, but also piles of school books. This was supposed to be a revision sleepover after all.

"Do come in Lau—" Fliss's mum greeted me at the door. I flashed her one of my looks. "... erm, Kenny. Now take your shoes off, there's a good girl. The others are already up in Felicity's room revising. Oh, I don't envy you girls, I really don't. I keep telling Felicity how very important these SATs tests are. I wasn't at all sure about having this sleepover you know. You will promise to work hard won't you L— Kenny dear and not lead the others astray, hmm? I know what a little bundle of energy you can be!"

She gave me one of her tight, false little smiles. So I beamed back with my broadest, most innocent grin. "Oh Mrs P, I wouldn't *dream* of doing anything silly tonight," I told her seriously. "Not when you've been good enough to let us have our sleepover here."

Mrs Proudlove looked at me with a funny expression on her face. Like she didn't know whether to believe me or not. She opened her mouth to say something, but thought better of it and gestured for me to go up to Fliss's room.

"What is your mum like?" I squealed as I burst through the door. "Accusing me of leading you all astray. As if!"

But if anyone looked like they needed to be led astray, this lot did. They were sitting in a row on Fliss's bed, seriously studying some maths worksheets and working out the answers in their little notebooks.

"Oh-oh, swot alert!" I groaned and dumped my stuff in the corner of the room. "It looks like I've got here just in time. Ten minutes later and you'd have turned into a right load of anoraks."

"We're just going over those maths problems Mrs Weaver set us," Fliss explained primly. "We *are* supposed to be revising, you know Kenny."

"Pardon me for breathing!" I retorted. "But there is such a thing as work overload, you know. There comes a point where your brain just can't take in any new information, so whatever you revise is a waste of time. There was a programme about it not so long ago."

Frankie put down her book. "You know Kenz, I remember seeing that too," she said seriously. "The presenter guy said that when that happens, you must stop working straight away, didn't he?"

"Yeah, that's right," Rosie chipped in. "'Cos if you don't your brain will explode for sure."

"How can you stop it happening?" Lyndz asked anxiously.

"Well," I explained. "He said that to get your brain cells working again, you absolutely must..." I produced my pillow from behind my back. "... have a pillow fight!"

I thwacked Frankie over the head and she went flying back on to the bed. She struggled to grab hold of Fliss's pillow then brought it crashing into Rosie.

"Hey watch it!" Rosie yelped, and rushed to grab hold of hers.

Soon a full-scale fight had broken out, with Fliss rushing between us squealing, "I really don't think we should. Please. Mum will go ballistic if she catches us."

Fortunately, the twins Joe and Hannah were in full-on howling mode downstairs, so Mrs Proudlove had more than enough to keep her busy without disturbing us. And by the time she did come upstairs to tell us that dinner was ready, we were all exhausted and had crashed out on the floor. Fortunately Frankie had heard her coming.

"Here, grab these," she whispered, dishing out the rather crumpled maths worksheets.

As soon as Fliss's mum came into the room, I piped up, "I reckon the answer to question seventeen is 'a rhombus'. Does everyone else?"

"Yep."

"Sure do!"

"Well girls, I'm so glad to see you're working hard," Mrs Proudlove beamed. "But I think it's about time you had a break for some food. We can't have you working so hard that you faint, can we?" Her silly little tinkly laugh wafted after her down the stairs.

"There wasn't a question seventeen, you dill!" Frankie punched me playfully on the arm.

"So?" I grinned. "It fooled Mrs P, didn't it?"

Now I don't know about you, but when I think of the kind of food I want after a hard day's revision, I think of pizza or fish and chips or jumbo apple pie with lashings of custard. I don't think of piddly little sandwiches and iced fairy cakes. No wonder Fliss is so thin, if that's the kind of food she gets to eat when she's working.

"If I had to estimate what fraction of my tummy is full after that meal," I whispered to Frankie, "I'd have to say two fifths at the most."

"Sssh!"

"And the probability of me keeping the rest of you awake all night with my rumbly tum is approximately a hundred per cent!"

Frankie by that time had dissolved into laughter.

"Is everything all right, girls?" Mrs Proudlove asked anxiously.

"Yes thank you," I nodded. "I was just wondering whether I could have another of your delicious cakes. I always find that working hard makes me very hungry."

"Of course, sweetie." Fliss's mum smiled and offered me the plate.

"Thanks," I said and scooped about three of them into my hand whilst I had the chance.

"So girls, do you think you'll be all ready for Monday?" Mrs Proudlove asked us eagerly. "I know you've been working extra hard, but you've just time to do a little bit more revision before bed. It will help your tummies settle down nicely."

I rolled my eyes at the others and we headed back up to Fliss's room.

"She's a bit of a slave driver, your mum," I moaned to Fliss. "Does she go on about the SATs *all* the time?"

"She just wants me to do well," Fliss snapped back.

"So does mine, but she kind of leaves the pressure off," Rosie admitted, pulling an apologetic face at Fliss.

"My parents," began Lyndz, "just say they want me to..."

"... TRY YOUR BEST!" we all chanted together and collapsed into giggles.

"Do you think we should just do a bit of science before bed?" Fliss asked quietly. The rest of us groaned and went to get our textbooks out of our bags. But the more we looked at them the less sense they made. The human skeleton, the food chain… it all blurred into one.

"Do you know what we need?" I shouted, jumping up. "We need something to completely take our minds off these stupid SATs. And what better than… gymnastics!"

The others didn't look too convinced.

"I'm not sure, Kenny." Fliss had gone white. "We promised our parents we wouldn't think about it until next weekend. Mum'll do her nut if she finds out we've been practising for the competition."

"But we *won't* be practising," I reassured her. "We're just going to let off some steam for a bit, you know. Clear our heads so that we're in a better frame of mind to study. What do you say?"

"Count me in!" Rosie was the first to leap to my side.

"And me," Frankie joined us. "As long as it's only for ten minutes."

"Well I guess I ought to start practising again," Lyndz admitted.

"OK then." Fliss got up from the bed. "But we will get back down to some work afterwards, won't we?"

"'Course," I agreed.

We pushed the beds to the side of the room as quietly as we could. Then we all started humming *Live and Let Die*. That made us crack up to start with because it sounded so funny. But once we got used to it, we started putting our moves together.

Fliss looked ace doing her routine and was as light as a feather when she landed. But Lyndz sounded like an elephant when she did her backward roll, even though she did it over her sleeping bag to cushion the sound.

"Mum's bound to have heard that!" hissed Fliss anxiously. But there was no sound of footsteps rushing upstairs, so we carried on.

The absolute best bit was when we started practising circle rolls as part of our routine all together.

"We'll go clockwise," Frankie suggested. But of course that didn't mean anything to Lyndz, who starts to panic whenever you mention clocks or watches. So there we all were rolling one way – and Lyndz rolled the other. Then Rosie changed directions too and soon we were a massive tangle of arms and legs. I started laughing so much I almost wet myself. And Lyndz got the dreaded hiccups, which just made the rest of us laugh even more. Tears were streaming down our faces and I was clutching my sides. I swear I was aching so much that I never thought I'd be able to perform another gymnastic move ever again.

It was really to stretch myself out that I started to cartwheel around Fliss's room. And when you're upside down you kind of lose direction a bit. How was I to know that Callum, Fliss's stupid brother, had been spying on us and had opened Fliss's bedroom door? So there I was, cartwheeling right out of the bedroom, across the landing and whoops, right into Mrs Proudlove's room.

The others were walking behind me chanting excitedly, "...13, 14, 15..."

When there was this almighty explosion.

I crashed to a halt – right in front of Fliss's mum, who was red in the face and screeching,

"JUST WHAT DO YOU THINK YOU ARE DOING?"

The others all bumped into each other behind me.

"I thought we agreed that there would be no gymnastics until *after* the SATs!" she continued. "I just *knew* that you couldn't be trusted. I should have known better than to agree to this sleepover in the first place. But what I *do* know is that your parents will agree with me when I tell them how you've abused our trust. There is no way now that you can be allowed to enter that competition."

Fliss virtually broke down in tears there and then and the others looked devastated. I felt kind of responsible, so it was up to me to think fast and save the day.

"Actually, you've got it all wrong Mrs P," I began innocently.

"I beg your pardon!" Fliss's mum went even redder in the face and looked as though she was going to burst for sure.

"We *are* revising, you see. We're looking at the way shadows are falling in front of me as I move."

"Yes, hic, that's what we, hic, do in science,"

Lyndz picked up my thread pretty quickly. "It means that the sun's, hic, behind her."

"And Kenny's not floating off into space when she cartwheels because of gravity," Rosie added seriously. "You see, the earth pulls all things towards it because of the object's weight."

Fliss's mum had calmed down, but she still didn't look too convinced.

"And we're using Kenny's display for English revision too," explained Frankie quickly. "It's sort of English in motion. 'Kenny's cartwheels cause chaos' – that's alliteration."

"And," Fliss piped up, "if Kenny did fifteen cartwheels and you multiply that by five you get..."

Oh-oh. Fliss wasn't really good at thinking on her feet. Her mother was looking at her intently.

"*Seventy five*," whispered Frankie behind Fliss's back.

"Seventy five," Fliss announced confidently.

"Hmm," Mrs Proudlove sniffed. "We certainly revised things differently in my day, but I suppose if it works it can only be a good thing. Just don't let me catch you performing your 'revision in motion' again, all right?"

We breathed a huge sigh of relief and headed back to Fliss's room.

"I think it might be an idea if you got ready for bed anyway," Mrs Proudlove called after us. "You're going to be needing as much rest as you can get over the next week."

"Don't remind me!" I hissed under my breath.

CHAPTER SEVEN

As soon as we were all ready for bed, we emptied our midnight feast on to the floor between us and sat up in our sleeping bags.

"I thought your mum was going to explode, Fliss," Rosie started laughing. "Did you check out her face?"

"I told you it was a bad idea to do gymnastics," Fliss replied huffily, but then started chuckling. "It was pretty cool the way we got out of it though, wasn't it?"

"A Sleepover Club classic!" I agreed.

As we chatted, we steamed into the sweets we'd brought. I'd never seen them disappear so quickly. Mini Mars, 'Tangfastics', toffee popcorn – they were all gone before you could flick-flack from one end of the room to the other.

"Your mum certainly doesn't believe in overfeeding us, does she Fliss?" I asked as I licked the last of the sugary bits from my fingers.

"She doesn't want me to get overweight, that's all," Fliss flashed back.

"Fat chance!" I retorted, which made everybody fall about laughing.

"Do you suppose plants ever get fat?" Rosie asked sleepily.

"Nah," Frankie replied. "They take all their nutrition through their roots, don't they? I guess they just take what's required to make sure the plant develops properly and grows as it should."

"It must be pretty boring being a plant," yawned Lyndz. "No pizzas, no sweets, just boring soil, day in, day out."

I couldn't believe what I was hearing. I mean, here we were on a sleepover and the others were talking about the growth system of plants!

"I'll tell you something," I said, snuggling down into my sleeping bag. "I'll be really glad when these SATs are over. We're turning into a real load of sad cases!"

By the time Monday morning came I was even more desperate for the tests to be over. As we sat in the classroom waiting for our first science paper, I felt sicker than I'd ever felt in my whole life. I really had worked hard for the SATs, I'd even surprised myself. But it was the uncertainty of not knowing exactly what kind of questions would be on the paper.

As we waited, we all gave each other the thumbs-up sign. Fliss was looking as white as a sheet and had dark rings under her eyes like she hadn't slept at all since our sleepover. I guess stress can get to you like that.

Mrs Weaver put the test papers face down on each of our desks.

"Now we've been through everything you're going to be asked, so read each question carefully before you answer. You have thirty-five minutes to complete the paper. You may begin."

I was actually shaking as I turned the paper over, and I had to force myself to concentrate on reading through the instructions. At first all I could see was the illustration for the first question. All the words underneath seemed to swim together. But I took a couple of deep breaths and read the question slowly. It was about identifying materials, which we must have gone over about a million times in class. And once I'd settled down, the questions themselves were pretty straightforward.

Actually the test wasn't as bad as I'd expected. Some of the questions were familiar and some were asked in a different way, so you really had to concentrate to work out what they were asking. The only one I struggled on was one about circuits, because you had to explain what would happen when the switch in the illustration was closed. I find it a bit difficult to write explanations like that down, but I tried my best.

I just had time to go back and check through all my answers before Mrs Weaver said, "Pens down please, your time is up."

As soon as she'd collected in all the papers we were allowed to go outside to the playground.

"Wasn't that just *awful*!" we squealed, collapsing into each other as soon as we got into the fresh air. We were mentally drained but kind of hyper as well. It was weird.

We went over the questions and asked each other what we'd put. I think we'd more or less got the same answers, apart from Fliss who by the sounds of it had done a different paper completely. She got a bit panicky actually, so we decided to give it a rest and run through a few gymnastic moves, just to calm ourselves down before the maths test in the afternoon.

It was well cool actually. I don't know whether it was because we were all pumped up by the SATs or what, but we all performed really well, even Lyndz.

"That was brilliant, Lyndz. You really nailed that backward roll," Frankie encouraged her.

Rosie had altered her routine and did a blinding handstand which she seemed to hold forever. Then she made a really smooth transition into a forward roll, finishing by standing tall and straight, just like a pukka Olympic gymnast. We were all amazed.

"That's brilliant," I gushed. "I've got a really good feeling about this competition now. Everything is going our way. We're going to win it, I know we are. I can feel it in my water!"

"Urgh Kenny, you're disgusting!" Fliss shivered.

"Well, can your water tell us what questions we're going to get in this maths test?" Frankie demanded. "Because I reckon we should do some more revision just in case your water can't be relied upon."

"Ha, ha!" I retorted. "But I guess you're right, as usual, Miss Thomas. It must make your brain hurt, being such a goody-goody all the time."

Frankie clutched her head dramatically. "It does," she moaned. "But I try to live with it!"

Giggling, we all ran back to the classroom to get our maths textbooks.

That gymnastics practice really helped to settle us down. So when it was time for the maths paper we were all chilled and totally prepared for it. And because it had worked for us that first day, we followed that pattern for the rest of the week. As soon as we'd finished one of our papers we ran outside and went through our gymnastics routine, then settled back to more revision. It was like a lucky talisman or something. You know, a kind of superstition, like those footballers who always do the same thing before each match because they think it helps them play better.

And do you know something? The SATs were really nothing to be scared about at all. Sure, there were some questions that were really hard, like calculating the perimeter of a star, or describing what happens when you use a forcemeter in science. But the others were just stuff we'd covered in class. The English comprehension paper was dead boring, though. I almost fell asleep in that test. They ought to have more exciting stories just to keep you interested, I reckon.

Anyway, we managed to practise our gymnastic routines every day, which we hadn't expected at all. And our parents couldn't accuse us of shirking our studies either, because the practices actually helped us. So by the end of the week, the SATs were all over and we had a full week ahead of us to perfect our skills for the competition.

"We're going to play a blinder in this gymnastics competition, I just know it," I told the others confidently. "We're way ahead of ourselves with our routines. If we rehearse to the max next week, we'll be international television superstars this time next month, just see if we're not."

Have you heard that expression about not counting your chickens before they're hatched? Well I was about to find out just how true that can be. Like being careful when you think you're standing on top of the world, because it just might start crumbling beneath you.

We had arranged to meet up at my place on Saturday afternoon to go through our routines, but somehow we'd conveniently forgotten to ask any of our parents if that was all right. Mum chucked a major wobbly as soon as I mentioned it.

"You know it's Grandpa Littler's birthday," she huffed. "And he loves it when we all get together for a party. You've got a whole week to practise for your competition, Kenny. I'm sure one day of not seeing your friends won't kill you."

The day might not kill me, but I was sure

that my friends would. But hey, shows how much I know. Because when I rang Frankie to tell her the bad news, she sounded positively relieved.

"No probs," she assured me. "Actually, we've got someone coming round to discuss some decorating, and Izzy's just not herself. I don't know what's up with her but she's really grizzly. I sort of promised that I'd keep an eye on her whilst Mum and Dad arrange everything with the decorator guy, so I'm kind of glad you've rung up to cancel."

Charming!

"Just you practise your routine as much as possible, OK?" I warned her.

It was the same story with both Lyndz and Rosie. Not about them having to look after Izzy, obviously. Lyndz's grandparents were coming over from Holland for a visit, so the whole family was in a mad panic trying to get their house into some kind of order. And you remember Lyndz's house, don't you? It's always in a state, so boy did they have their work cut out! And Rosie was going to Alton Towers with her dad and his new family. He'd planned it as a surprise for her after the SATs. I know that she feels as though she misses out on stuff since he left home, so I kind of felt happy for her.

"You just make sure you come back in one piece, OK?" I teased her. "No falling out of Oblivion, or else there'll be big trouble."

"A big mess, you mean!" Rosie joked.

Before I could even get in touch with Fliss, Mrs Proudlove was on the blower herself, panicking as usual. I heard Mum trying to calm her down and promising that Dad would pop round just as soon as he got back from surgery.

"What's up? It's not the twins, is it?" I asked when she'd finally got off the phone.

"No, it's Fliss," Mum explained. "She has a headache and is very weak and faint. I'm sure it's nothing serious but your dad will sort her out, don't worry."

Sure enough, when Dad came in he said she was overtired and he'd prescribed lots of rest and no excitement for the next few days. No excitement! Didn't he know we had an appointment with destiny to keep? I mean, the gymnastics competition was about to change our whole lives.

'OK, OK, stay calm," I told myself. "This is just one day. We've got a whole week to practise. Rosie will be back from Alton Towers, Frankie won't have to look after Izzy, Fliss will get better... I just hope Lyndz's family manage to tidy their house."

But life isn't that simple, is it? By Monday Fliss was still too ill to come to school and Rosie had been sick all weekend too.

"Mum said it was too many hot dogs and too many fast rides," she mumbled. I had to admit that she was still looking rather green about the chops. And Frankie was looking none too clever either.

"I'm just so worried about Izzy," she explained. "She's been screaming constantly for two days and her temperature's ever so high. I know Mum and Dad are really worried about her too. I think Mum's taking her to see your dad today."

At least Lyndz was OK.

"Anyone fancy doing some gymnastics?" I asked hopefully at breaktime.

Frankie and Rosie both shook their heads, but Lyndz and I went through a few moves. The trouble was that it wasn't easy practising them on the grass behind the playground. For a start the grass had just been cut, so when Lyndz tried out her backward roll, she got covered in green cuttings and looked like a mouldy Abominable Snowman! And another thing was that we didn't want anyone finding out what we were practising for. So whenever anyone came near us, like the dreadful duo, the M&Ms – our deadly rivals Emma Hughes and Emily Berryman – we had to collapse on to the grass and pretend that we were just having a general chat about pop music and stuff.

"Phew, we can't go through that again," I gasped, brushing the grass from my skirt. "From now on we'll have to practise after school at one of our houses. How about tonight?"

"Count me out," Rosie said. "I'd puke for sure if I had to do a cartwheel."

"And I want to get straight home to see how Izzy is," Frankie explained.

"Well what about tomorrow then?" I tried to stay calm. "You do realise that the competition is only four days away, don't you?"

"Erm Kenny, remember my grandparents are staying with us for a couple of days," Lyndz told me sheepishly. "And I've promised that I'll be home early for the next few evenings. Sorry."

"I don't believe this!" I yelled to the sky. "We've got this one chance to change our lives and we're going to blow it!"

When I got home I was still really mad at the others.

"Fliss rang a few minutes ago," Mum called out as soon as I'd walked through the door. "She sounded quite anxious, could you give her a ring?"

Phew! At least Fliss was taking this seriously. I mean, she was more desperate to get on TV than the rest of us put together. I knew that she wouldn't let me down.

"Wassup?" I yelled when she answered the phone.

"Costumes!" she squealed. "What are we going to wear for the competition? We haven't even *thought* about that yet, and it'll be the first thing the judges notice."

"Hey, hey, hey, don't get your frillies in a fix!" I told her. "I think what we're going to wear is the least of our worries right now. The rate we're going we won't even have a *routine* to show off, never mind any costumes."

I explained how the others hadn't been much use on the gymnastics front.

"That's *terrible*!" she gasped. "I mean, they need all the help they can get, don't they? At least I've been practising my bit whenever Mum's not around. She'd kill me if she found out. Your dad said I had to have complete rest."

"So when do you think you'll be back at school?" I asked.

"Thursday or Friday, Mum says."

"You're joking! That hardly gives us any time to rehearse together."

"I know, I'm really sorry. What about the costumes though? I'd thought maybe we should get pink leotards or something."

"No way!" I yelled. "Besides, we've no time to shop for anything new now. I guess we'll just have to wear the black leotards we sometimes wear for PE."

"Yucksville!" Fliss groaned. "No-one will even notice us in them."

"Well, the way things are going, the only reason anyone will notice us at all is because we look like a load of no-brain wallies!"

"I'll be back as soon as I can Kenny, honest," Fliss tried to reassure me. "In the meantime you'll just have to practise as much as you can with the others."

But that was certainly easier said than done. Frankie was in such a state worrying about Izzy for the next couple of days that she either completely forgot her routine, or else got it all out of synch and bumped into everyone else. Rosie did what she could but her tummy was still a bit dodgy, and she looked as though she could throw up at any moment. And Lyndz had to shoot off every afternoon to spend time with her grandparents.

It was only on the Friday that we were finally all together and everyone was in a fit state to rehearse. We all went back to my place after school.

"I'm so glad Izzy's better," Frankie told us as we were changing into our leotards. "It was only a bug, but she was really poorly."

"And I'm glad that *I'm* better too," Fliss said seriously.

"And *I'm* glad that you're all better, you're all here and we're all able to rehearse our routine," I snapped. "Now are you all ready? We haven't got much time left, you know."

I stuck *Live and Let Die* into the cassette player and cranked up the volume.

"And hit it!"

Talk about disaster! We all started moving at different times. Rosie went one way, Lyndz went another, and Fliss was so busy pouting and posturing that she ended halfway up Frankie's back.

"Come on guys," I shouted. "Let's try it again."

This time Lyndz tripped up and knocked into Rosie, who ended up flat on the floor.

"Are you doing this for a laugh?" I screamed. "Because it's not very funny."

"It is from where I'm standing!" Molly was creased up in the doorway.

"MUM!" I yelled. I had enough to contend with, without having to deal with my evil sister as well.

Once Mum had dragged her away, we started again. That time things weren't too bad. All right, I'll admit it, it was me who messed up the routine when I misjudged a cartwheel.

"It'll be OK tomorrow, we'll have more space," I said, struggling out of the armchair.

"I hope so," Frankie mumbled under her breath.

We rehearsed and we rehearsed. Then we broke for a quick sugar fix, and we rehearsed some more. Three hours later the others were all begging to go home.

"We'll be exhausted by tomorrow," Rosie moaned. "We need a rest. Please Kenny, the last few times the routine's been OK, hasn't it?"

"Hmm."

It was OK, but I was sure we could do better.

"Just once more through then."

That time, despite being dead tired, we performed like stars.

"Do it like that tomorrow and we're on our way to a television series for sure," I beamed.

As Fliss was getting changed she suddenly pulled a whole load of shiny badges from her bag.

"I almost forgot, I made these for you," she grinned. "They're on a sticky backing so they won't spoil our leotards."

They were the letters SC in silver on a shiny pink heart-shaped background.

"Mum helped me make them when I was ill," she explained.

"Cool!"

"I think we've just got ourselves a lucky emblem," I laughed. "Right guys, I'll meet you at the Leisure Centre bright and early tomorrow morning. Don't be late!"

When I went to bed later, I was so pumped up I just couldn't sleep. And when I did get to sleep, I had this crazy dream about the floor at the gymnastics competition turning into toffee and Fliss being eaten by a great big marshmallow. Talk about weird. I'd definitely been working too hard!

The next morning as I waited for the others to arrive at the Leisure Centre, I felt quite sick. Not as sick as I'd felt before the Science SAT, though. It was a sort of nervous but excited feeling, if you know what I mean. And my nerves certainly weren't helped by the fact that there were already *hundreds* of girls milling about in their tracksuits and leotards. There were a few boys too, but it was mainly girls. And do you know something else? They were all absolutely *tiny*!

"Blimey! Look at the size of everyone!" Frankie gasped as soon as she arrived. "I'm going to stick out like a sore thumb here, aren't I?"

I caught sight of Rosie pushing her way through the crowds. She looked really relieved when she spotted us.

"It looks like everyone else wants to be television stars too," she pointed out.

Fliss and Lyndz soon joined us. Lyndz looked completely terrified by the number of people there were, but Fliss lapped it up. She had this look of supreme confidence, which said, *I'm better than you, so don't you forget it*!

As soon as we were all there, we joined a queue of other girls waiting to get inside. And once we were at the front we gave our names to a woman with a clipboard. Another woman showed us to a section of the main hall that had been screened off as a warm-up area.

"You're in Group One in the first competition area," she told us.

Apparently there were two sets of judges simultaneously judging competitors on two exercise floors. They would each choose five groups who would go on to the proper final the following weekend.

"Look, there's a camera over there!" Fliss suddenly shrieked excitedly. "It's just like *Popstars*!"

A camera crew was moving around the edge of the warm-up area, filming people going through their paces. Some girls were completely ignoring them and doing the most amazing stretches, you know, with their legs behind their ears, or doing the splits on the floor.

"They've got to have done this before," Rosie whispered.

Other girls were crowding round the cameras and the presenter from the local news.

"Look, we'll just have to ignore them and get on with practising our own routine," Frankie told us seriously. "We're never going to win this competition if we don't even warm up."

We stripped off to our leotards and followed her on to the warm-up area. I was kind of used to stretching out because of all the sports I play, but Lyndz and Rosie were looking a bit lost.

"Just do what I do," I hissed, and stood on one leg pulling my other foot to my bottom.

"This stretches out your quads," I told them.

"You what?"

"That's the muscle down the front of your thigh, dimbos!" I grinned.

Fliss meanwhile was trying desperately to look as though she stretched out every day of her life. As the rest of us started to run through a few of the moves from our routine, she flew over to us in a fluster.

"The camera crew is coming this way!"

Sure enough, the presenter was heading straight for us. We tried to act all cool and relaxed. But it wasn't easy when Fliss was dribbling with excitement.

"Hi girls, I'm Julia Ward," the woman smiled at us. "Would you mind if I had a quick chat to you about the competition?"

For a few seconds we all froze with terror.

"Nah, 'course not," I grinned. "As long as you don't mind Fliss cracking your camera!"

Fliss smacked me, the cameraman started laughing and that was it really; there was no stopping us.

"So what made you enter the competition?" Julia asked.

"Well it keeps us out of mischief," I replied, straight-faced.

"You're not kidding. Kenny's been making us practise for *weeks*!" Lyndz sighed, and Rosie and Frankie pretended to faint with exhaustion.

"Even when I was *really* ill I kept practising," Fliss told her seriously. "We really want to win the competition you see, because..."

The rest of us were mugging away and pulling faces behind Fliss's back but Frankie suddenly turned into Mr Sensible.

"What Fliss means is that we're really looking forward to entering the competition for the experience," she explained. "Being part of the whole thing is much more important than winning."

Fliss flashed her a look, but Julia seemed very impressed.

"And just one last thing, girls. I see you're wearing badges with 'SC' on them. What does that stand for?"

"The Sleepover Club!" we all shouted back.

"Well it's been great to meet you." She

turned back to the camera and said, "We'll look forward to seeing the Sleepover Club later, but now let's see some of the groups already performing.

"Bye girls!" she waved as she followed the camera crew to the arena.

"That was amazing!" Fliss gushed. "Just think, we're going to be on telly!"

"I don't know about that, but the competition's already started, look." Frankie pointed to our competition area. "We'd better run through our routine one more time and then watch some of the others. It might be our turn soon."

The warm-up area was pretty deserted with most other groups crowding round one of the two arenas. The routine seemed to go pretty OK, although of course we didn't have the music to guide us.

"You have got the cassette, haven't you Kenny?" Fliss asked me for about the millionth time.

"No, actually I've just eaten it, Fliss," I snapped back. "'Course I have. Will you stop panicking?"

But I guess we all started panicking a bit when we saw the other competitors in action. Some of them were amazing, performing really complicated moves with backflips and flick-flacks and everything.

"We don't stand a chance, do we?" Rosie moaned.

"They're looking for raw talent," I reminded her. "Some of these people look as though they've been going to gym class since they were in nappies, and that's not what the competition's about. They're trying to encourage new people to take it up, remember."

"Well I hope you've noticed that everyone else is performing to show tunes," Fliss hissed nastily. "If they don't like our music, it's all your fault."

"I bet the judges are bored out of their brains by show tunes now," I told her. "They'll be really relieved to hear something different."

"Well we're about to find out," Frankie told us. "The woman over there has just called for 'The Sleepover Club' to come forward. We're on next!"

It's hard to describe how I felt as we were waiting to run out into the arena. Part of me was really fired up and I wanted to punch the air and yell, "Bring it on!" But part of me wished I could run away. Because the hall had been divided into two areas there wasn't much room for spectators, so the only people watching were other competitors. But that made it worse in a way, because they obviously wouldn't be wanting us to do well.

We held hands as we waited for the woman to announce us, and as soon as we heard, "And our next competitors are – The Sleepover Club!" we ran into the middle of the floor together.

Julia Ward was standing at the side with the cameraman. She gave us a big grin and a thumbs-up sign.

"They're not going to be filming us, are they?" Fliss whispered under her breath.

"Dunno, but give it your best shot," I whispered back.

I handed our cassette to a woman and we took up our starting positions. Suddenly the music boomed out. I think it was a bit of a shock to most people because it was so different. It was almost as though you could hear everyone gasp. But, and I know this is going to sound kind of stupid, we could feel a sort of buzz coming from the audience. And soon everyone's toes were tapping for sure.

We tried to pretend we were just performing for ourselves and that nobody was watching, which kind of calmed the nerves a bit. I performed my solo routine first and it was pretty darned perfect. My walkover-cartwheel combo was spot-on, even if I say so myself. That kind of gave the others a boost and Frankie did just about the best arabesque and forward roll I'd ever seen her do. And even I have to admit that Fliss was absolutely brilliant. She was like a gazelle and went about a mile in the air when she did her stag leap.

Rosie was next, and when she held her handstand I thought she'd never come down again. She never wobbled or anything, but I think she was so pleased with herself she missed her cue for her forward roll which meant she was late finishing her solo.

Poor Lyndz. She was worked up about things beforehand, but when she realised that she'd have to start her routine before Rosie had quite finished hers, you could see the panic spread across her face. She looked just like a rabbit caught in the headlights – scared is the understatement of the year!

Actually, old Lyndz was really very good in the end. Her log-roll went a bit off-course though and her 'SC' badge came unstuck and dropped off. She hesitated a bit before sitting up, not quite knowing whether she should pick it up or not. But she didn't, and followed straight through with her backward roll. Unfortunately the badge decided to re-attach itself – to the top of her head.

Rosie saw it first and started to splutter. Then I realised what was up, and had to swallow hard so I didn't start snorting with laughter. Somehow we all got through our circle roll finale, which went down a storm. By the time we finished I swear that everyone was cheering much louder for us than they had for anyone else.

"Did you hear that?" I gabbled excitedly

when we'd taken our bows and run off. "The crowd loved us!"

"We're bound to be picked for the final now, aren't we?" Fliss gushed. "And the camera crew is coming over too! That's got to be a good sign!"

Julia Ward was full of praise for us, and we chatted and laughed about how nervous we'd been. I was on such a high that I can't really remember *what* we talked about. Or for how long. All I do know is that it only seemed a couple of minutes before someone told us that the judges were going to announce which groups would be going through to the final.

"Is it OK if we stick with you and film your reactions?" Julia asked us.

"Of course it's OK!" Fliss beamed smugly. Then she whispered to the rest of us, "We're hardly going to refuse to have our moment of glory captured on film, are we?"

My heart was almost bursting out of my chest as the chairperson made a speech about how impressed they'd been by the standard of competitors, and how it gave her confidence for the future of gymnastics in this country.

"And finally the moment you've all been waiting for..."

She read out five names which we didn't even recognise.

"They must have been the ones in the other group," Frankie whispered.

Then she started with names from our part of the competition. Every time she spoke, my heart beat even harder. I was sure you'd be able to see it popping out of my chest. I don't really remember the camera filming us, but I do remember us all clinging to each other and Fliss chanting, "Please let the next one be us!"

By the time there was just one more group to announce, Fliss was clinging to my hand so hard that I'd lost all feeling in my fingers.

"And finally," the chairperson announced. "The last group to go through to the final is... The Sleep..."

CHAPTER TEN

"... The Sleeping Tigers!"

Just for a second there, I really thought we'd won. In fact Fliss had already leapt off the ground before she realised it wasn't us. A cheer went up from the back of the hall – it was from one of the groups of boys. They were all jumping around, punching each other and doing high fives.

I turned to the others. They were looking dead miserable and Fliss had big tears welling up in her eyes. Unfortunately there was still a great big camera pointing right in my face. I'd almost forgotten that we were still being filmed. It wasn't going to look good if we were big cry-baby losers, now was it?

"Well," I looked straight into the camera. "I guess we were just too good for this lot!"

Julia Ward laughed. "Aren't you disappointed that you haven't got through to the final?" she asked. "Wouldn't you have liked the chance to learn to do gymnastics properly and be filmed at the same time?"

We all looked at each other.

"Nah!"

We cracked up laughing, although Fliss was still looking a bit tearful and wobbly.

"We've really had a great time and everything," Frankie explained. "But to be absolutely honest, gymnastics is much harder work than we thought."

"You're not kidding!" I agreed. "We're absolutely *exhausted* now."

I stuck my thumb in my mouth and pretended to fall asleep on Fliss's shoulder.

"Gerroff!" she shrugged, but even she had started laughing.

"But at least Lyndz has discovered a new hair accessory," I said seriously, and pulled my

SC badge from my leotard and stuck it on my head.

The others did the same and we started striking mad model-type poses in front of the camera.

Julia Ward was cracking up, but she managed to say, "Well girls, although you didn't win, you've certainly given us a lot of pleasure."

Then she turned to the camera and said, "Now let's go and interview some of the successful finalists."

She gave us a wave and mouthed, "well done" before heading into the throng of excited bodies crowding round the judges' tables.

"I know they've filmed us and everything, but do you think we will appear on TV?" Rosie asked wistfully as we watched Julia interviewing other people.

"I doubt it," Frankie said. "It'll only be on the local news for about a minute, so I bet they'll just concentrate on those people who've got through."

"I hope so," Lyndz sighed. "I look really awful in this leotard."

We collected our stuff and walked out of the Leisure Centre.

"Look guys, we might not have won, but it's been an experience hasn't it?" I asked. "We've been filmed even if we don't end up on television this time. I mean, at least when we do get the chance to appear on TV again, we'll know what to expect. We'll be like old pros!"

"But I wanted to appear on TV *now*," Fliss groaned. "It's so unfair."

"No it's not, Fliss. The others must have been better than us, that's all," Frankie reasoned. "I mean, we're not exactly natural gymnasts, are we?"

"Nope," Rosie admitted. "But you were right before, Frankie. All that gymnastics lark *was* too much like hard work. Let's face it, none of us are really cut out for it, are we?"

Fliss sniffed and narrowed her eyes meaningfully.

"Not even you Fliss," Frankie agreed. "You're much more model material, aren't you?"

Fliss grinned and admired her reflection in one of the shop windows we were passing.

Frankie raised her eyes at the rest of us and we had to stifle our giggles so as not to give the game away.

"Anyway guys, there are two good things as far as I can see," Lyndz began seriously. "The first is that I can finally do a backward roll properly..."

We all cheered.

"... and the other is that we've got another sleepover to look forward to. It's round at your place at four, isn't it Kenny?"

"Sure is," I grinned. "And we've no SATs to revise for, and no gymnastics to practise. Tonight girls, we're just gonna have fun!"

Whooping and yelling, we all ran down the road like loonies. And it kind of carried on that way round at my house later. In fact we only flopped down in front of the television in the middle of the evening because we were so exhausted after charging round in the garden playing crazy chasing games.

"Aw no, it's the news, bor-ing," Rosie moaned as I channel-hopped.

"Turn it back Kenny," Frankie ordered. "The gymnastics competition should be on."

I flicked back. Sure enough, after a report on escalating car crime, there was Julia Ward at the Leisure Centre.

"This is it!" we all squealed. "Can anyone see us? Is that you, Frankie?"

We squinted at the screen trying to pick ourselves out from the background.

"Quick, record it Kenny, just in case."

I didn't have time to find a new videocassette so I slammed down the record button and prayed that whatever was on the video already in the machine, it wouldn't be one of Dad's precious documentaries.

"Look, look!" Fliss suddenly shrieked. "It's us!"

And there we were, in full colour. It showed the interview before our performance, with us messing about and pretending to faint and everything. Then there was just a tiny glimpse of our performance in amongst loads of clips of other people's.

"You'd think they could have shown all of ours," Fliss tutted.

"But we didn't win Fliss," Rosie explained. "Oh no, here we are again."

That was the bit with us listening to the results and larking about afterwards.

"I don't believe it!" Lyndz grinned. "They featured us more than anyone else, even though we didn't make it through to the final."

"Star quality you see!" I grinned. "The offers will be pouring in now."

We started to pretend that we were appearing in our own television series, until we were interrupted by Molly the Monster.

"All right saddos, clear off. I'm going to watch the programme Mum recorded about Robbie Williams now and you're not, so GET OUT!"

We all looked at each other, and at the video recorder. Oh-oh. Time to make ourselves scarce! We raced up to the bedroom as fast as we could and locked the door behind us. Sure enough after about ten seconds there was a banging on the door, accompanied by Molly screaming:

"You did that on purpose didn't you, you evil little cow! I'm going to kill you for this! And all your stupid friends too!"

It was class! I couldn't have planned it better if I'd tried. Mum gave me a telling-off about being irresponsible and I had to apologise to Molly (puke) but it was still worth it just knowing how fuming she was.

We had to keep a pretty low profile for the rest of the evening. But even that was cool because we paraded about in my bedroom pretending we were TV stars. And of course we had to have the inevitable run-through of our gymnastic routine one more time – or one hundred and one more like!

But the absolute *best* thing was that when we got to school on Monday morning we were treated like superstars. Everyone had seen us on the television and they all wanted to know what it was like. Kids from Year One came up to us and just stared at us like we were great big international film stars or something. Brilliant! And the ultimate highlight was that we got right up the M&Ms' noses because they couldn't bear us having so much attention. When Mrs Weaver asked us to tell the rest of the class all about our experiences you should have seen their faces! They went so red with anger that I thought they were going to explode all over the classroom.

The whole thing was totally, totally wicked. And even though we didn't win the competition, we'd only entered it in the first place so we could get on television and that had certainly come true.

Fliss of course is sure that some big talent scout is going to sign her up at any moment and give her her own TV show, but that's Fliss for you. The rest of us are just thrilled it worked out like it did. Even Lyndz, because although I don't think she'll ever make a gymnast, she's much more confident in PE now. And of course the fame thing is wicked – we're milking it for all it's worth. We've got to get into practice, you see, so when we're major stars we can take it all in our stride.

I can't believe now that we almost didn't enter the competition because of the stupid SATs. It seems such a long time ago since we did them. We're trying to forget about them actually because we won't know how we got on 'til summer. At least we all tried our best, so that should keep our parents happy.

Anyway, I'd better go now to sign more autographs for my adoring fans. I can't keep them waiting, you know.

Catch ya' later, dude!